I know something that you don't

by

MELISSA KLIMA

authorHOUSE™

1663 LIBERTY DRIVE, SUITE 200
BLOOMINGTON, INDIANA 47403
(800) 839-8640
WWW.AUTHORHOUSE.COM

This book is a work of fiction. People, places, events, and situations are the product of the author's imagination. Any resemblance to actual persons, living or dead, or historical events, is purely coincidental.

First published by AuthorHouse 04/29/05

ISBN: 1-4208-4635-3 (e)
ISBN: 1-4208-4634-5 (sc)

Printed in the United States of America
Bloomington, Indiana

This book is printed on acid-free paper.

Chapter One

"There is never a place to park in this stupid parking lot. Can't some of these people just go home," Sara complained as she kept circling the lot intensely scanning each car hoping to see her chance for a spot. "Oh, there we go. Come on, grandpa, get a move on. Come on, come on, back it out. There you go. Old people are so annoying. They shouldn't even be allowed to drive," she mumbled to herself as she pulled her brand-new white Tahoe into the now open parking space. As Sara put her truck in park, she snatched up her purse and quickly opened the door to get out. She began her trek across the parking lot toward her favorite coffee shop. The smell of spring was all around her, but she didn't notice it. To her dismay, the melting snow had created many puddles of dirty water, which her high-heels had now splattered across the back of her legs. "Damn it," she said as she

1

cranked her head around her shoulder to take a look down at her pants. "I just bought these and now they're filthy and probably stained. How am I supposed to enjoy spring when this is what I get?" Annoyed and frustrated now thinking of the extra trip she'd have to make to the cleaners, wondering if they'd even be able to get the stains out, she continued walking toward the coffee shop.

"For the love of God," she exhaled. "Now I forgot my duffle bag in the back seat." She whipped herself around and headed back for her truck. Sara had to get her duffle bag. That bag contained all her problems, all her stories about her life. Her past, her present and her future were all inside. She never went anywhere without it. Sara opened up the back door of her Tahoe. She wrestled with her duffle bag pulling and tugging on it to get it out. Finally, she managed to throw it over her shoulder. "Holy Hanna, this thing has gotten huge and it's so heavy. I can hardly carry it," she whined. "I might have to get one of those wheelies pretty soon." Just then a woman next to Sara shut the door to her car. She too had her very own duffle bag and with ease and grace she tossed it up upon her back as if it weighed nothing at all. "Hi there," the woman said with a friendly smile. She then looked up to the sky and back down again at Sara. "What a beautiful spring day. Life is good," she said.

Sara gave her a quick grin. "Yeah, right, whatever," Sara thought to herself. "You must be on some good drugs lady."

The woman continued to smile at Sara and before walking away, she commented, "Your duffle bag looks quite heavy. Do you need some help with it?"

"Oh, no. I'm fine. Thanks anyway. I've got it," Sara replied.

"Okay. Have a nice day," the woman said politely as she walked away.

Now alone by her truck, Sara wondered how that woman could be so happy. "I want a lighter duffle bag too. I want a bag that's fun to carry around. I want to be happy like her, but how," pondered Sara.

Chapter Two

"I'll get that for you," a delightful gentleman said as he held the door open for Sara to enter the coffee shop. "You've got your hands full. That's quite a bag you've got there."

"Yes, it is," sighed Sara, "and I'm really tired from lugging it around too."

"Hey, Sara," said a familiar voice. "I'm over here." There was Tammy. She stood up and waved Sara over. Sara and Tammy had been long time friends, way back to the college days. Sara walked over and pulled out a chair at the round table next to Tammy. "Wow," Sara said as she put her bag down next to Tammy's, "your bag is as big as mine."

"Yes," said Tammy, "I have lots to tell you."

"Me too," Sara said, "but I'll let you go first."

Tammy reached down and unzipped her bag. She shuffled through all the problems and stories searching for the one she wanted to take out first. "There it is," she said, "my trophy problem. I'll start with this one." Tammy placed her biggest problem on the table.

"Wow," said Sara, "that's a big one."

"I know. Can you believe he did that to me?"

"You poor thing. This must be just awful for you."

Over the next hour, Sara and Tammy took turns setting their problems on the table. Carefully, they analyzed and discussed each one. It was now time to wrap things up, so they each returned their problems and stories to their individual bags. As Sara and Tammy were saying their good-byes, Sara recognized a woman who was sitting quietly in the corner of the coffee shop reading a book, peacefully enjoying herself. "Oh, yeah," Sara thought to herself, "that's the happy lady who offered to help me outside in the parking lot with my bag."

Just then Tammy interrupted Sara's thought. "Do you see someone you know?"

"Well, I don't really know her," Sara replied. "I met her in the parking lot right before coming in here to hook up with you. She was really happy and look at her bag, it's so small and light. I'm just wondering if she knows something about life that we haven't figured out yet."

"Well, let's go ask her," said Tammy.

"No, I don't even know her."

"So what," replied Tammy. "Let's just go ask her. Besides, my back is starting to really hurt from carrying my duffle bag around."

Eagerly, Tammy walked over to the peaceful woman in the coffee shop. "Hi," Tammy said as she put her hand out for the woman to shake. "I'm Tammy and this is my friend, Sara."

The woman instantly smiled and rose up to greet them. "What can I do for you two lovely ladies?"

"As you can see, our duffle bags have gotten quite large and heavy and yours is so small and it looks as light as a feather. We were thinking that maybe you know something about life that we don't know."

Again the woman smiled. "What exactly would you like to know?"

"How to be happy," Sara interrupted. "We want to know how to be happy."

"Pull up a chair," the woman said, "and I will share with you the secret of happiness."

Chapter Three

Tammy and Sara quickly sat down and so the woman began. "I'm going to be really straight with you here. If you want to have a life that's full of happiness, if you want to walk from this coffee shop to the end of your life enjoying yourself and feeling good about who you are, not to mention waking up in the morning and being glad you're still alive, then you better be ready to hear some things that might hurt your feelings a little. I'm going to give you the straight facts about who you currently are and the hard cold truth about your behavior and how that "it wasn't my fault" attitude of yours is ruining your life. I will not criticize you. I will be honest and straight forward without any fluffy stuff around it about why your duffle bag is so heavy and why you're not as happy as you'd like to be. This conversation won't be about what you're currently doing that is working for you. It will be about what you're doing that is not working for you. I will tell you exactly how to get what you want and you will clearly understand why you couldn't get it before.

First of all, I know exactly how you are. You make promises all the time and then do a half-ass job following through with them. You say you'll be there at 6:00 and you show up at 6:15, 6:30 loaded with your excuses and justification as to why you were late. "I forgot that I had to get gas." "There was a hitchhiker and he needed a ride, and I felt sorry for him because it was snowing out." "I put my dog in his kennel and I locked myself in with him for hours. He has diarrhea right now. It was a nightmare." And one of our all-time favorites, "The traffic was terrible. The city really needs to do something about our freeways. It was a parking lot out there." And last but not least, "I'm always late and I just can't help it. I guess it's just the way that I am." Every time you're late, you justify it.

Or… you take on too much at work because you're the "yes, I can do it" person and then you don't get it done. And when you don't get it done, you have your excuses and justifications for that too. "I would have gotten it done, but Sally gossips so much at work and I have to listen to her, even though I don't like gossip." "My computer crashed and I lost everything." "I'm having personal family problems and I just can't talk about it because I'm just too emotional right now." "My cat is dying and he's at the vet and because of that,

I went out and drank way too much, but it's not my fault that I didn't get it done." "I don't know why, but I just can't get things done lately. I'm a procrastinator. It's just the way that I am." Every time you don't get things done, you justify it.

And to top it off, you have your excuses and justification as to why you're the "yes, I can do it" person in the first place. "I had to say yes because I might lose my job if I didn't." "I had to say yes because I'm a nice person and nice people always try and help out." "I had to say yes because the word "No" is just too negative of a word." "I had to say yes because I always say yes. It's just the way that I am." Every time you say yes, you justify it.

Now we absolutely cannot overlook this one, it's just too popular and too painful to skip. "Yes, I lied but it was just a little lie. Your lie was a big one, at least mine was a little white lie." "I had to lie because if I told you the truth, you would get mad at me." Or how about this one? "I had to lie because if I told you the truth, it would hurt your feelings." Every time you lie, you justify it.

How about being crabby, also known as being negative, also referred to as being a bitch, also called being a prick, another way to say it… I'm unhappy and my life sucks or I'm just plain old depressed. Oh, yes, these are good ones. There isn't a human being alive who can't relate to these. "I'm really in a bad mood because I had a horrible day at the office." "If I had a different job, I would be happy." "The kids have been fighting and arguing with each other for hours and I'm just really irritable because of it." "I wouldn't have said all those awful things to you if you hadn't started it first. It's because of you that I'm so negative. In fact, if it wasn't for you, I would be happy." "I can't stand the way you drive. Whenever you drive, I get really annoyed." "My dad is an alcoholic and because of that, I'm unhappy. It's so hard being around him." "My grandma died and I've been miserable and depressed ever since." "You know, I have everything and I'm still not happy. It's just the way that I am." Every time you're unhappy, crabby, negative, bitchy, depressed or acting like a prick, you justify it.

The reason I'm so good at creating all these excuses and justifications and explanations is because I used to carry them all around with me in my bag. I have lied on so many occasions in the past that I can't even count them, nor would I try. I have said yes to things and then never completed them. There were times when I agreed to something and I knew full well that I could never follow through with it, but instead of just saying that, I lied and agreed to do it only later to explain and justify what happened. I have been late. I have been depressed. I have been crabby, negative, unhappy and even a prick. There was a time when my duffle bag was as big and heavy as yours.

Have I made my point here on justifications, excuses and explanations? Can you see in your own life how you justify and explain absolutely everything you do, how everything is because of something? I'm not saying it's a bad thing to justify your behavior either. It's not a bad thing. I'm just asking you if you can see that you do it.

Chapter Four

Now here's an important question, do you have any idea how attached you are to your justifications? Well, let me tell you something, you are VERY attached. They have become your whole life. Let's think about this one. When a friend or someone you know tries to help you let go of your justification or excuse and they offer a healthy and positive perspective on one of your problems, what do you do? I know exactly what you do. You try even harder to convince them and explain to them why you are the way you are and how impossible it would be to fix the problem. You get really passionate about your story. You get very defensive. You'll even fight for your story about why you can't and why you are just stuck with your situation and then you'll go into how it's not your fault.

Your friend or whomever you're talking to has basically two choices at this point. They either agree with you because they can tell you're not going to let it go or you've been so passionate that you've actually convinced them to see it your way; or they can continue to encourage you to improve your situation. If they do take a stand for you and continue to offer positive suggestions, guess what you do, you get annoyed with them and you get irritated with them. You even get snotty with them for not agreeing with you. You may even consider at this point that maybe they're not such a great friend after all. You may even end the friendship and then, once again, you justify it by saying, "She just doesn't understand me. She is so annoying. She thinks she's better than me. She has no idea what I've been going through." Or you'll just say, "You know, I have to get going. I'm real busy at work. Let's just talk about it later." You absolutely, without a doubt, believe that your justifications are real and are very much alive, and you are very passionate about keeping them. You are very protective of your justifications. They make perfect sense to you and you fully, absolutely, without a doubt expect that everyone in your life should understand them.

So why is it then when someone is late, you're annoyed? You say, "How disrespectful of him to be late. That guy is rude." But when you're late, you justify it and everyone is supposed to understand. You say, "Well, yeah, I've been late but not as much as him. He's always late. I'm only late once in a while." And somehow your justification is better than his?

Why is it when someone doesn't get something done, you're irritated with them? You say, "My kids just don't get their chores done around the house." "My husband always starts these projects, but never finishes them. It drives me crazy." But when you don't get things done, you justify it and everyone is supposed to understand. You say, "I might not finish everything around here, but it's because I have to take care of the kids." And somehow your justification is better than theirs?

Why is it when someone lies to you, you feel completely betrayed? You say, "I just can't trust you now. How could you lie to me?" When someone lies to you, you completely forget that you've ever lied yourself because you become such a victim. And when you do remember your own lies, you justify them by saying, "Well, yes, I've lied but it was a white lie and it wasn't as big of a deal as yours. I mean, when I lied, we weren't even married yet" and everyone is supposed to understand. And somehow your justification is better than theirs?

Why is it when someone is rude to you, crabby or negative you find yourself feeling really hurt or the opposite, you want to be really mean back? You say, "He was so rude and negative to me. I just can't tell you how he has hurt me." But when you're rude and negative, you justify it and everyone is supposed to understand. You say, "I might be being rude and negative, but it's because he was negative first. I'm rude and negative because I've been around him so long." And somehow your justification is better than his?

Why are your justifications better than other people's justifications? They're not. You just think they are. The truth is you justify your behavior and then you judge others for their behavior. You act like their justifications mean nothing. Let me tell you something, their justifications for their behavior are just as real to them as your justifications are to you. Everybody out there is doing the exact same thing, justifying! So when you judge others for their behavior, what you're actually doing is being a hypocrite. In actuality, you are what you say you hate. You are what you complain about, you're just justifying why it's okay for you to be that way.

So now that you're aware that you justify everything you do, that others justify everything they do, the fact that you judge others for doing the same things you do, now is the perfect opportunity for you to give the people in your life that you love the most, or even those you don't like at all, a break. They are not awful, self-centered, negative monsters like you may have thought. They are just like you and I, they are just busy justifying everything they do. I am not asking you to agree or disagree with their justifications. I am asking you simply to respect their right to have them, whatever they are.

This is a good time to realize and acknowledge that there are some people in your life you could apologize to. Call them up, write them a letter, do something to get rid of that grudge you've been dragging around with you, get rid of that worthless justification about why you're not close with someone anymore. And be generous with your apology too. Let that certain someone vent to you for a while about how you have hurt them and then apologize again, apologize generously. They may not forgive you right away either and that's okay. It may take some time for them to digest that you really are sorry. Or, maybe there's someone you've lost touch with and your justification is "I've been too busy to call." Give them that call and tell them you've missed talking with them.

Once you've done this, once you've cleaned up a mess with someone, you are actually opening up a space in your duffle bag. You now have some room in there for something new. This is your chance to fill that space with a problem that's worth having, a problem that's worth talking about, a problem that is to your advantage, like "I started doing foster care and I have a new child in my home." This is a problem worth talking about because you're benefiting someone else's life by taking a child in who needs you. Create some problems that are worth hauling around with you. Turn your trophy problem into a problem that you can be proud of.

I want you to be really clear on something before we go on. Life is all about carrying around your duffle bag and that's a good thing. It's what's in your duffle bag that determines how happy or unhappy you are. What's in your duffle bag? What's your trophy problem? What do you want to keep hauling around with you and what are you going to throw in the trash?

Are you now capable of seeing that the only thing between you and what you want in your duffle bag are your justifications, your excuses for why you can't? Your justifications, your excuses, are the only things that are weighing you down . You are the one who decided they exist. You are the one who decided they were real. You are the one who created them. And because you are the creator, then you have all the power. You can do with them what you want. You are responsible for what's in your duffle bag.

If the things in your life that you're not happy with are someone else's fault, you have no power. Every time you blame someone else, every time you point your finger at someone, you lose power. If your bad marriage is your husband's fault or your wife's fault, you are a sitting duck with your hands tied. When anything is someone else's fault, then you're just waiting around powerless, complaining and hoping someone comes in and fixes it and saves the day. Think about it. You're going to be waiting a long time for your life to get better because you just put your happiness on the shoulders of another.

Answer this question for me: What are you willing to give up to be right that things are not your fault? What are you willing to give up to keep justifying why you can't have what you want? I'll tell you what you're giving up, you're giving up EVERYTHING. Say good-bye to a happy marriage because you're going to be waiting for your spouse to fix it. Say good-bye to well-rounded respectful children because you're going to be waiting for their teacher or someone else to fix them. Say good-bye to great friendships because you're going to be waiting for your friends to see that nothing has been your fault. Say good-bye to a close relationship with your parents because you're going to be too busy blaming them to have the time to love them.

Let me tell you something. If you have a bad marriage, it's your own fault. If your kids are disrespectful and out of control, it's your own fault. If you don't like your job, it's your own fault. If you don't have any friends, it's your own fault. Everything, without exception, that you complain about is your own fault. You are responsible for your duffle bag and what's in it. Now that might not be what you want to hear and you may be screaming, "It's not my fault though because, because, because." But the truth is, you want it to be your fault. Because if it's your fault, then you have the power. You can fix anything that you take responsibility for and you can make it whatever you want it to be. Are you understanding that if you're to blame, that's a good thing because then you have all the power you need to create a wonderful life?

This is another perfect time to realize that there are some people in your life that you could apologize to. Call them up, write them a letter, do something to get rid of that grudge you've been dragging around with you, get rid of that worthless justification about why you're not close with someone anymore. Be generous with your apology. Let that certain someone vent to you for a while about what their story is and then apologize again. Or, call someone up who you haven't talked to in a while. If you want to be closer to your dad, call him up and tell him that. It's that easy. Go beyond your justifications about why you can't and just do it. When you do this, when you clear up a problem with someone, you instantly lighten your load. You can be proud of yourself because you took charge and made your life better. That big heavy duffle bag isn't quite so heavy anymore. You're the one who has to carry it, so do yourself a favor and think about who you could call.

You might be thinking at this point, "Yeah, that makes sense, but I am not going to apologize to him. He was such a jerk to me. This is his fault, not mine" or

"I'm not going to call up my dad and ask him to have a close relationship with me. He's the one who should be calling me," and you're off with all your justifications again about why you shouldn't have to and how you're not to blame. And what do you get when you think this way? You get something in return. There is a reward when you act like a victim. There is a reward in waiting for someone else to say they are sorry first. What is the reward exactly? You're thinking, "What are you talking about? I'm not getting any reward." But you are. You get to be irresponsible and not get things done, not to mention something to talk about with your friends that's really juicy and interesting. But best of all, what really matters most to you… you get to be right. You get to be right that it's someone else's fault. You get to be right that you and your dad are not close and it's his fault. You get to be right that you have a bad marriage. You get to be right that you can't stand your sister. You get to be right that your mother's pathetic. You get to be right that you haven't talked to your brother in two years. You get to be right that you have an unfulfilling life. You are right!

Do you want to be right? Really ask yourself, "Do I want to be right about my story?" What are you willing to give up to keep being right? Currently, at this very moment, you are sacrificing your happiness and the happiness of everyone that matters to you all so you can be right.

Chapter Five

The biggest question ever asked is, How do I do it? I want a happy life. I want a passionate relationship with my spouse. I want to be close to my children. I want a job that I love. I want to be right about some really great stuff, but how do I do it? The good news is, you're already almost there. You understand that you justify everything. You understand that the other people in your life justify everything. You understand that everyone is really attached to their justifications, that they think their justifications are real. You understand that it's not your place to judge others because that makes you a hypocrite. You understand that you don't have to agree or disagree with other people's justifications but simply respect their right to have them. You understand that being responsible and seeing where you're to blame is where the power is. Every time you point the finger at someone, you give away your power and put your happiness on their shoulders. You understand that you will always be carrying around a duffle bag and what's in it determines how happy or unhappy you are. You understand that by apologizing and asking for a close relationship with someone, you put something in your duffle bag worth hauling around with you. You know more right now than most people will ever know.

But just to really enlighten you, I'll give you the last piece of the puzzle. What in your life is factual and what in your life is optional? What do you have a choice over and what do you not have a choice over? There's two things in your life. And yes, it's that simple. There's the facts, also referred to as the events of your life. And there's your feelings, also known as your story. So we have facts/events and we have feelings/your story. The facts/events of your life are absolutely separate from your feelings/your story about them. Let me give you a visual so you're crystal clear on this." The wise woman held up two sheets of paper and this is what they said.

FACTS/EVENTS	FEELING/YOUR STORY

"See that they are separate. Seeing that they are separate will literally give you your life back. You will become completely empowered by mastering this skill.

Let's go over the facts of your life first, the events that have taken place. The first fact is, you were born. That's just a fact. We're not going to place any feeling to that for now. We are simply acknowledging the fact that you were born. I'm sure you have lots to say about that, but we're sticking to the fact that it occurred right now." This time the wise woman held up three sheets of paper and this is what they said.

FACTS/EVENTS	FEELING/STORY	FEELING/STORY
I was born	I'm glad I was born because, because, because	I wish I was never born because, because, because

"You can't change the fact that you were born, but you sure can create lots of different stories about it.

Death is a fact, an event that will occur whether you like it or not. We have many feelings and stories about that event too, but the event of death is separate from your story about it.

Another fact is, you have a body and a face. Some people may say you have a pretty face and some people may say you're quite ugly. Maybe you love your body, maybe you hate your body. But the fact is, you have a body and a face and how you feel about your body and face is separate.

Divorce is an event. Everyone has their own feelings about divorce. Some say, "I love being divorced. Best thing I did." Others may say, "I hate being divorced. It's been so hard on the kids and on me." Someone may even have such a horrible story going on in their head about divorce that they would rather murder their spouse than divorce them. It's their story that drives them to commit such an act. But regardless of anyone's story, divorce is simply a fact, an event. Are you seeing how important it is to separate your story from the event?

FACT/EVENT	FEELING/STORY	FEELING/STORY
Divorce	I love being divorced. It's worked out for the best	I hate being divorced. I'm ashamed of it.

Divorce is just an event, you get to choose your story. You are responsible for your story.

Marriage is an event. Some say, "I love being married because I didn't like being single." Some say, "Marriage is boring because you never have sex anymore." The fact is, marriage is just an event. Your story about it is separate.

Your children are an event. Now I know you have tons of stories and feelings about your children, some good and some not so good, but your children are a fact, an event. You are the creator of the stories you tell about them.

Religion is an event. An event that people create such passionate stories about that they even kill each other over it. Of course they justify killing people by saying, "It's because you don't believe in what we believe in and our religion is the right one." But religion is an event. Your story about it is separate.

A few more events are flying, food, money, college, Christmas, your car or truck, your job, your mother, your house, taxes, mowing the lawn, cats, dogs, your birthday; these are all examples of events.

I can keep going over a million different facts/ events here. Can you see yet what in your life is a fact and how your feelings and story about those facts are separate? Your feelings may jump on top of the event so quickly that it's hard for you to see the difference, but they are definitely separate. This is an important part and I want to make sure you see the facts and events separate from your feelings and your stories about them. Practice seeing the events in your life as just that, events. Do not attach any emotion or feeling to them. Once you've accomplished that, listen to what your story and feelings are about them. Acknowledge that your story and feelings are separate from the actual event.

You have no choice over the events in your life that have already occurred. They just simply are there. The events that have happened in the past are done. They simply happened. You do, however, choose how you feel about those events. Your feelings and the stories you create around them are 100 percent optional. How you feel about those events is up to you. You get to choose how you feel. The events are just there, but you choose how you feel about them. No one makes you feel anything. You decide that all by yourself. You are responsible for how you feel. I've heard people say many times, "You can't help how you feel." And that is ridiculous. That is the biggest line of crock I've ever heard. You can create any story you want to about any event in your life and that's a fact.

Now you're saying, "I didn't choose to get divorced and have my life fall apart." "I didn't choose to get laid off. Of course I feel bad about it." "I didn't choose to be depressed for two years after my brother died." "I don't choose to be afraid of flying. I don't like being scared." "I didn't choose to be annoyed with my mother-in-law. She is annoying." "I didn't choose to be angry after my husband had his affair." Well, yes, you did. Remember, taking the blame is where the power is. Divorce is the event, but you chose to let your life fall apart. Getting laid off is the event, but you chose to feel bad about it. Get off your butt and find another job. Stop justifying why you can't. Death is the event, but you chose to be depressed for two years. Flying is the event and you chose to be afraid of it. You can chose to not be afraid of it just as easily. The rewards in not being afraid are much higher than the rewards for being afraid. Flying and enjoying it is much more fun. Maybe you have to choose to enjoy the ride ten times that day but keep choosing to your advantage, keep justifying why you enjoy it. Your mother-in-law is just that, she's an event. You choose to see the worst in her. You choose to backstab her and what does that make you? You didn't make your husband have an affair, but you get to choose how you feel about it. Now you're really thinking I'm crazy, but it's true. I met a woman who said to me, "My husband having an affair was the best thing that ever happened to us. We are so close now because of it." Here's the deal, if you create nasty, negative, pathetic, depressing stories about the events in your life, you get a reward. You get to be irresponsible, you get something to complain about and you get to be right.

You can argue with me all you want, but it doesn't change the fact that you choose how you feel. And you know what? You want to choose how you feel. If someone tells you how you feel, do you like that? No, you say, "Don't tell me how I feel. It's my life and

I know how I feel." Exactly! It's your life and you decide how you feel.

A friend of mine says, "Marriage is boring." He really believes it too. He will flat out argue with you and defend his story about why his marriage is boring. He will completely fight for his worthless story. And guess what? He gets to be right. His marriage will be boring for the rest of his life. He gets to put that in his duffle bag every morning and carry it around. Everyone who knows him can see that it's his own fault, but he can't. He has a beautiful and spontaneous wife, but he's so busy justifying that he is absolutely blind to all that he has. When she does something romantic and sexy, he puts his nose up to it. He is choosing to give up a loving, passionate marriage to be right about his story. Of course, he has no clue he's choosing this story. To him, it's just real. He has no idea what you have figured out, that your stories about events are optional. You get to pick them. You are responsible for what's in your duffle bag.

How about being able to walk? Walking is an event. Are you so busy justifying why you're depressed that you forgot to be deliriously happy about the fact that you can walk? Walking is a big deal. Christopher Reeves knows all about that one. He spent the last nine years of his life as a quadriplegic after a fatal horse-riding accident. He could have easily chose a "poor me" story, but instead, he chose to focus on what he could still do, not on what was taken away from him. He didn't have a choice over the event of being paralyzed, but he did have a choice over how he felt about that event. Reeves became the Chairman of the Board of the Christopher Reeve Paralysis Foundation, CRPF, supporting the research of effective treatments and a cure for paralysis, not to mention a long list of other contributions. Christopher Reeves is an inspiration and he always will be. You too can take the events in your life and use them to empower yourself.

Try this one on. "I used to love my job and now I don't. I'm not excited to go to work anymore. My performance is way down. I'm not sure why. I guess I've lost my edge." No, you haven't lost anything. You just changed your story about the event of work.

"I have a question for you," said Tammy. "You don't choose who you love though, right?"

"Oh, my sweet girl," replied the woman, "yes, you most certainly do. You choose to love and you choose who you love.

"But when I fell in love with Joe, it just happened. I'm quite sure I didn't choose that," Tammy argued.

"What's your explanation for it then, some magical love dust floated down from the sky and created your destiny?"

"Yeah, pretty much," Tammy answered realizing how foolish that sounded. "It's more like he swept me off my feet."

"Well," the woman said, "it makes sense that your bag is so heavy. Being a victim of love really weighs you down. It's not Joe that makes you love him. It's your story about Joe that makes you love him and you created that story. Therefore, it's because of you that you love him. You choose to put Joe in your duffle bag. The wise woman took out four sheets of paper and wrote on them. She then held them up and this is what they said.

FACT/EVENT	FEELING/STORY
Joe	I love Joe because, because, because
FEELING/STORY	FEELING/STORY
I hate Joe because, because, because	

"Why is the last sheet blank?" Tammy asked.

"Because it's up to you to create any story you want to about the event of Joe. You are never stuck with your story. You always have a blank sheet to create whatever story works for you. You are always right about your story. Whatever you create for yourself, you will be right about. What do you want to be right about?

You are responsible for your stories and justifications. You actually created them. Yes, you made them all up yourself. You can choose any story you want about any event in your life. If you feel like you don't have a choice over your feelings/story, then you are still choosing it by default. Either way, you're still responsible and either way, it's still a choice.

Chapter Six

Let's take a quick minute to discuss the justifications and stories that do work well, the kind that keep your bag light and easy to carry around.

"My dad is an alcoholic and seeing the pain that that caused our family growing up, I choose not to be a drinker. I forgive my dad for being an alcoholic because I know waking up every morning being addicted must be so hard for him. I can't imagine what it would be like to panic at the thought of not drinking. He's been to treatment twice now. He hasn't been able to kick his addiction yet, but I am so thankful that he's tried. I always tell him that he can do it no matter how bad things get. His behavior has saved me. Because of him, I'm not an alcoholic."

"My mom didn't give us much attention when I was little, so now I'm a great mom because I don't want my kids to go through that. I see now why it was so hard for her to give us attention. She had so much on her plate back then. I am thankful for what she did do. Considering what she had going on, she did a great job." Choose to focus on what your mother has done for you, not on what she hasn't. Being mad at your mom for not raising you like you think she should have is like being mad at your dishwasher because you wish it was an oven. How silly would you look complaining to people about how your dishwasher is just a dishwasher and how you're mad and sometimes even sad because you really want it to be an oven? "I'm so upset with my dishwasher. I just wish it could be an oven. I've told it a million times how great being an oven is and it just doesn't listen. If my dishwasher could just be an oven, then I would be happy." That's how silly it is to complain about your mother. She is what she is, she's your mother. Your dishwasher is what it is, it's a dishwasher. Complaining about your dishwasher won't make it an oven. Complaining about your mother, won't make her a better mother, but it will make you unhappy and it will weigh your duffle bag down. Appreciate your dishwasher for what it is. Appreciate your mother for what she is. Choose your mother the way she is.

"When my spouse comes home crabby, I am nice because I know how it feels to be crabby." When you're crabby, do you feel good? No, you feel terrible on the inside. It's no fun being crabby. You're not running around giving everyone hugs because you love being crabby. You're miserable and you don't like it. So when someone is crabby to you, be nice to them. Give the crabby people out there a break. Instead of getting irritated by their rudeness, just ignore them or if you want, ask them if they're okay, ask what's bothering them. You might be surprised by their response. You may even turn a crabby person into a friendly person.

And my all-time favorite justifications are, "I am responsible for my life because I know that's where the power is." "I am responsible for my life because it isn't someone else's job to make me happy." "I see the good in people because it's fun trying to find it and thinking good thoughts makes me happy."

Take the justifications in your life and turn them around to your benefit. Create stories and justifications that work for you. Because when trash comes out of your mouth, trash is what you are. Every time you start complaining about something, this is your opportunity to see the opposite of your complaint. You may say, "I hate rush hour traffic." You now have the wisdom to see the opposite. "I don't mind rush hour traffic because it gives me the opportunity to unwind from a long day and listen to my favorite music." You are going to be in rush hour traffic anyway, so you might as well enjoy it. Some people have created such negative stories about the event of other drivers that we now refer to it as road rage. Are you seeing yet how important it is to recognize the difference between an event and your story about it? Why don't you give the guy in front of you a break. Maybe he just found out his wife has cancer. Maybe he's cutting you off because he's worried that he's going to get fired if he's late and he just found out his girlfriend is pregnant and making money has now become really important. I guarantee you he's not a jerk. He's just like you, he's carrying around a heavy duffle bag trying to make it in this world.

When you say, "My husband doesn't give me enough attention," now is your opportunity to say, "My husband gives me lots of attention. I just didn't give him any credit for the attention he did give me before. Every time he mows the lawn, that's his way of saying I love you." Think of all the ways your husband says I love you that you've just been putting your nose up to, all the wonderful things that you don't even bother to say thank you for anymore. Think of all the blessings in your life that you've been spitting on as if they have no meaning at all.

When you say, "Work was so stressful, I need to go to the bar and have a drink," now is your chance to say, "Work was so stressful, I need to go work out at the club." Drinkers justify why they drink and non-drinkers justify why they don't. When you say, "I'm a worrier. It's just the way that I am," now you can say, "I'm not a worrier anymore because worrying is a waste of time." When you say, "I yell at my kids because then they listen," now you can say, "I talk calmly to my kids because then they listen. I used to yell at them, but that just made them afraid of me." Instead of getting caught up in what's right versus what's wrong and who's right versus who's wrong, just simply ask yourself, "Does what I'm currently doing work for me?"

Admit it, you are an excellent storyteller and you are very passionate about creating justifications. So keep on telling stories and keep on justifying them, just do it to your advantage. If you're as stubborn about justifying why your life can be and is great as you are about justifying why your life can't be and isn't great, I promise you that your life will improve dramatically. It will take practice at first, but soon it will flow from you naturally. I mean, if you're going to fight for something, fight for your happiness and start seeing the good that life has always had to offer you. Imagine how good you're going to look and sound to others. Your friends and family are going to want to know how you figured out how to be happy and love your life again because -- yes, the good old because -- because everyone wants to be happy. They're just not sure how. You can't always choose the events in your life, sometimes life lifes you, but you do choose how you feel about those events. Choose wisely. The stories you tell are your reality.

All your life is, is a bunch of stories about the events in your life. And remember, you may have to choose happiness more than once.

Chapter Seven

I'm going to leave you with one last tidbit of wisdom. I want you to think back to a time when you felt really happy, life was good and you felt really content and peaceful. The good news is, that didn't just magically happen to you. You actually created the story that made you feel that way. You were responsible for it! You justified why you were happy, and justifications are optional, which means you chose it, you just didn't realize it. You have the ability to feel really happy, peaceful and content any time you want. It's always there for you. All you have to do is drop your negative story and pick up a positive one."

"But how do you do that?" asked Tammy.

The woman took a pencil and handed it to Tammy. "Drop the pencil to the floor," she told her.

So Tammy did, she dropped the pencil and it landed on the floor.

"How did you do that?" asked the woman.

"I just did."

"Exactly! You just drop your story like you dropped the pencil, you just do it. Now why did you drop the pencil?"

"Because you told me to drop it."

"And why would you drop a negative story?"

"Because it makes me unhappy."

"Exactly!" said the woman. "You've got it!"

The woman rose from her chair, gave the girls one last smile and said, "God gave every one of us freewill, also known as voluntary choice, the freedom to decide. He promised to never take that away from us and he hasn't."

Tammy and Sara just looked at each other for a while in silence. Then Sara burst out laughing and giggling, and then Tammy burst out laughing too. "I just can't believe it," said Tammy with tears in her eyes from laughing so hard. "I had no idea I was the one making my bag so heavy. The joke's on me!"

"Life is so simple," Sara added, "and I made it so complicated. It's no wonder I'm overweight, just look at the stories I've created about myself and about food in general. My new story about food is that it's for survival, not for comfort. Working out and eating healthy gives me comfort. I get to choose my feelings and stories. Thank you, God, for freewill."

Chapter Eight

"See you Thursday," Tammy said to Sara from across the parking lot."

"See you then," replied Sara. After tossing her duffle bag upon her shoulder, it dawned on Sara how light her bag had already become. She stopped for a moment and took in a deep breath of fresh spring air. "I forgot how much I love spring," she thought to herself. She continued walking toward her truck and once again, her high-heels kicked up specs of dirty water across the back of her pants. This time, instead of getting mad, she started to dance around in the puddles of water fully appreciating the fact that she could. She reveled in the warmth of the sun and spun her body around and around.

"What are you doing?" asked a thin frail man who had stopped to observe Sara's behavior. He stood with his arms crossed and a wrinkle of judgment overtook his brow.

Startled by his presence, Sara fumbled with her answer, "I'm, I'm, I'm dancing."

"I can see that," said the man in a gruff voice. "Do you realize you're dancing in a puddle of mud?"

"It's not a puddle of mud. Actually, it's a puddle of spring," she explained with a smile. Just then Sara noticed the man had a red wagon sitting next to him. Curiously she asked, "What's in your wagon?"

"It's my duffle bag," he replied. "It's gotten so heavy that I just can't carry it around anymore, so I found this here wagon to make it easier on myself. I finally figured it out," he said as he winked at Sara. "I have to ask you though," continued the man, "what makes you so happy that you would dance around in a puddle of mud?"

Sara started to giggle again. "Because of coffee," she explained as she pointed to the coffee shop.

Chapter Nine

S ara set her duffle bag down next to her and leaned back up against her truck. She knew the dirt from her Tahoe was going to cover the back of her shirt, but she chose not to care. She wanted to take a moment to let all that she had learned soak in, and she realized that being so uptight about staying clean had caused her unnecessary stress. She thought of all the times she had yelled at her kids for getting dirty. It dawned on her that they weren't rude, inconsiderate little monsters trying to make her life more difficult. That was just her story. What they really were, were little kids having fun and she had become the rude, inconsiderate monster by yelling at them. "I'm going to apologize to them when I get home and I'm going to play with them and get dirty myself," she decided. "A little dirt never hurt," she whispered giggling at herself.

As Sara continued staring off into the parking lot doing a little duffle bag watching, she began thinking about her father. She always wanted a close relationship with him but blamed their lack of closeness on him. Another light bulb went off in her head. "I've been complaining about how my dad doesn't do anything to have a close relationship with me but actually he does. I've just put my nose up to it. I've spit on the cards he's given me for my birthday. I've spit on the love that he's offered me because I thought it wasn't good enough, but it is good enough. He's done the best he can and I'm the one spitting on his best. I am what I've been complaining about. I'm the one who's not doing anything." Sara was so excited that she jumped in her truck, grabbed her cell phone and called up her dad.

"Hi, dad, it's me."

"Well, hi there, Sara, is everything okay?"

"Yeah, everything is fine. Why?"

"Because I usually don't hear from you unless something's wrong."

"You're right, dad, and I want to apologize to you for that."

"Oh, that's okay. I like to hear from you no matter what you're calling about."

Sara's eyes filled up with tears. "I want to be closer with you, dad, and I was wondering if we could get together for lunch next week, like on Monday maybe?"

"Monday doesn't work, Sara, I'm just too busy that day." Sara's heart sank. "How about Friday?" her dad asked.

"Friday is great. I'll juggle some stuff around to make it work. And dad, I'm really uncomfortable about saying this, but I'm going to say it anyway, I really love you."

"I love you too, Sara. You know, you sure are happy today. What is it you've been up to?"

"I met a friend for coffee."

"You should have coffee more often. This is the best talk we've had in years."

As Sara hung up the phone, she rolled down her window and yelled to a stranger passing by, "I got my dad back today!"

The stranger smiled and gave Sara a thumbs-up. "Good for you," he shouted.

Sara rolled up the window and started her truck. "I don't want to be right anymore about not being close with my dad. If I'm going to be right about something, I'm going to be right that we are close and whatever that takes, I'm going to do it. That woman is right, this taking the blame stuff is really fun. I want everything to be my fault!"

"Now I'm going to call my ex-husband. Boy, am I going to make his day." Sara dialed John's number. "Hi, John. It's Sara. I want to talk to you about something. Are you busy?"

"Yeah, I'm busy. What do you want?"

Sara was feeling nervous at this point but decided to have faith in what the wise woman had suggested. "Well, I want to apologize to you about some stuff."

John was completely taken aback by Sara's words. Their divorce had been quite a battle, not to mention an ugly custody dispute over their three children. John was definitely not used to Sara being polite and friendly to him.

"Did I hear you right? You, the most bull-headed person on the planet, want to apologize to me, the guy you say ruined your life? Sara, are you drunk?"

"No, I'm not drunk."

"Well, did you and your new husband get in a fight or something?"

"No, we're doing fine. I just want to say I'm sorry for some things I've done."

"Well, I have all the time in the world for this conversation. What's going on?"

Sara took a deep breath. "First off, I want you to know that our divorce wasn't all your fault. I can see now that you did some really nice things in our marriage and I didn't appreciate them."

"It's a little late to be sorry now, Sara. Things between us are a disaster and I'm not going to let go and just forgive you for all the mean and hurtful things you've said and done just because you say you're sorry."

"John, we've both said hurtful things to each other."

"Maybe so, Sara, but you have been way meaner than me. I was only trying to protect myself and you're the one who wouldn't agree on anything during our divorce."

Sara felt a strong urge to fight back and stand up for herself, but she remembered that taking the blame is where the power is. She didn't want to give up a healthy relationship with her ex-husband so she could be right anymore. It just wasn't worth it. Who was right and who was wrong didn't matter. Finally, she could see beyond her story about John and she was more than ready to create a new one. She knew it was up to her to make that happen. "You're right, John. I was hard to get along with during the divorce and during our marriage. I don't blame you for holding a grudge against me. You are entitled to your opinion. I may not always agree with it, but I do respect your right to have it. I just want to tell you that I'm sorry for hurting you. I'm sorry for being rude and I'm sorry for lying to you. I hope in time you'll be able to forgive me and let go of the past."

"I do appreciate you saying that, Sara. I'm not quite sure I believe you, but it does feel good to hear you say it. For the kid's sake, I think it's best if we get along. They shouldn't suffer because of our problems."

A warm peaceful sensation moved throughout Sara's body. She felt a huge sense of relief, all because she took the blame and apologized. Sure there were still issues, but Sara wasn't about to spit on what just happened. She was extremely thankful for the progress they had made. One small step is actually a really big step. Sara was proud of herself and she had every right to be. She took the path of being responsible, a path that always leads you to happiness.

"Thank you for taking the time to talk with me, John. I know how busy you are and I also want to thank you for paying child support. I always just expected it from you before and I've never bothered to tell you how much I appreciate that you do pay it."

There was a pause of silence and then John replied, "You have no idea how nice that is to hear. I realize it's the law and that I have to pay you, but knowing you appreciate it sure makes paying you a lot less irritating. I wish I could talk longer, but I have to get going."

"No problem," Sara replied, "I'll have the kids call you tonight before bed so they can tell you about their day."

"I would really like that," said John and they each hung up the phone.

"This is so cool," Sara thought to herself. "I always thought taking the blame was a bad thing. I avoided it like the plague but boy, was I wrong. For the first time in my life, I actually want to be responsible."

Many names and faces crossed Sara's mind as she thought of all the different people in her life that she could call and apologize to, not to mention the old friends she had lost touch with. Then she thought of her friend Tammy and wondered if she had called and apologized to anyone yet. Sara was already looking forward to their coffee get-together next Thursday. She couldn't wait to share with Tammy all the new stories she had created and to show off how light and easy to carry her duffle bag had become.

Sara scrolled through her cell phone to her current husband's number. She pressed the send button and anxiously waited to hear his voice, craving for him to answer his phone. Early that morning she and her husband Steve had gotten into an argument. As Steve was getting dressed for work, he had turned the light on in their bedroom abruptly waking Sara from a deep sleep. Sara was not happy about it either and she let

Steve have it for waking her up. She couldn't believe how rude and inconsiderate he had been. After all, they had a three-month-old who still wasn't sleeping through the night. I mean, how self-centered could Steve be to not think about what it was like for Sara to be awake all night while he just took care of himself.

After the third ring, Steve finally answered. "Hi, Sara, what's up?"

"Oh, I'm so glad you answered your phone. I am so sorry for being so awful to you this morning. I created this dreadful story about you because you woke me up. I really believed that you were being disrespectful and rude and selfish and inconsiderate, but actually you were showing me you loved me. You were going to work and you got up early because you love me. You are so ambitious and caring and loving, and I'm the one who was disrespectful and rude and unappreciative. I'm so sorry I thought those things about you because you are absolutely the best thing that's ever happened to me. You didn't turn the light on because you're selfish. You turned the light on because you wanted to match your socks up with your suit because you're a great guy who works really hard. I'm so sorry. Will you forgive me?"

"Of course, I'll forgive you. I'm thrilled that you realize there's more than one way to look at things."

"I totally get that now," replied Sara, "and I'm so pumped up about it that I can hardly stop smiling. I'm just bubbling up inside."

"You know, Sara, I could use a flashlight in the morning to find a pair of socks that match. I very much appreciate that you get up with the baby and I know you need your sleep."

Sara was pleased with how well the conversation was going. It was obvious that taking the blame opened up doors that once were shut. "That's kind of silly, but I think it actually would work. Then you get your socks and I get my sleep," Sara laughed.

"There's something else I want to talk to you about," she continued. Before Sara and Steve were married, they dated for about a year and a-half. During their dating days, Steve had cheated on Sara with another woman. He very much regretted it and he had begged Sara to forgive him. After many tears and long hours of discussion, she decided to forgive him for that mistake, but she had never forgotten it. Even after they were married, this topic came up numerous times and had continued to be a sore spot for Sara. Even though it was in the past, it still negatively affected their relationship. One of Steve and Sara's biggest issues were trust. Sara struggled on a weekly basis, if not daily, with whether she could trust Steve. She wasn't sure how to trust him after being betrayed like that, but she knew she still loved him. "Well, honey," Sara began, "I have figured out the solution to my trust issue. You cheated on me in the past and it's over and done with. I have been the one keeping it alive by carrying it into our future together. It will always be a memory, but I can find the good in it. There is good in even the worst events. The good thing is, it made you realize how much you adore me. And if that's what it took for you to see that I was the one for you, then so be it. I'm not going to be mad at the dishwasher. I'm just going to revel in the fact that you adore me."

"Why would you be mad at our dishwasher?" Steve asked completely confused.

"I'll explain that part later. So anyway, I understand now that trust is a feeling, which makes it optional, which means I have to choose to trust you. Before today, I was waiting for trust to float down on me like a magic powder. That may sound crazy, but I didn't understand that I had to choose it. I have to choose to trust you, just like I choose to love you, just like I choose to eat breakfast, just like I choose to take a shower. I was blaming you and what you did for my inability to trust you, and there's no power in blaming you, my hands were tied. The truth is, I am responsible for my trust issue. I justified why I couldn't trust you and now I'm going to justify why I can. I'm going to choose to trust you because I want to be happily married. I want our marriage to be a success. And in order for that to happen, I need to choose feelings that match up with that goal. I may have to choose to trust you more than once, especially when those negative thoughts come creeping in, but I will keep choosing to trust you. And if you were to cheat on me again, then so what. The world isn't going to end, the traffic isn't going to stop, my life wouldn't be ruined because of it. I don't want you to cheat on me, so please be clear about that, but I'm not going to spend my precious energy worrying about it anymore. I am, however, going to spend my precious energy on doing things for our marriage that will improve it. No more checking your cell phone when you're not looking to see who you've talked to, no more snooping through your coat pockets and underwear drawer. I'm done with all that. I'm going to take the time I would have spent checking up on you and use it to do nice things, things that will create a happily married couple. I'm going to choose to be vulnerable and give you everything I've got. I'm so excited! I just love being responsible!"

Steve was overjoyed with Sara's new-found wisdom. "Wow, I'm so impressed with you, Sara. You can count on me to do the same. Being vulnerable isn't something most people are comfortable with, but it's the only way to really feel love, to experience that full-blown, pitter-patter, I-just-got-to-have-you, my-whole-body's-tingling, loving feeling.   So what made you understand all this?"

"I met Tammy for coffee today, you know, it's Thursday and we always meet for coffee on Thursdays, and we met this really wise woman and she explained it to me in a way that I could actually understand."

"What was her name?"

"I guess I don't know. I forgot to ask her. Wow, there I go again being rude and inconsiderate, and I didn't even see that I was doing it. She helped me make sense out of my life and I didn't even bother to ask her what her name was."

"Well, did you tell her thank you at least?"

"No, I didn't even say thank you. You know what, Steve? I really love you and I can't wait to be with you tonight, but I'm going to hang up with you for now and head back over to the coffee shop. I want to see if that woman is still there."

About the Author

It's taken over thirty years and a lot of experience, but Melissa Klima has finally mastered the secret of happiness. She is delighted to share the secret with you.

"Life can be really tough sometimes, but you're in good hands now. I wish I could be there to see the expression on your face when you finish reading my book and to watch your life dramatically improve. I'm so excited for you!"

Melissa Klima lives in Minnesota with her husband and their three children.

Printed in the United States
29893LVS00001B/91-189

9 781420 846348